The Owl and the Pussycat

For Annie,
PJ and
Jamie
K.W.

SIMON AND SCHUSTER
First published in Great Britain in 2010 by Simon and Schuster UK Ltd
1st Floor, 222 Gray's Inn Road, London WC1X 8HB
A CBS company

ISBN: 978-1-84738-348-8 (HB)
ISBN: 978-1-84738-349-5 (PB)

Printed in Singapore
2 4 6 8 10 9 7 5 3 1

The Owl and the Pussycat

by Edward Lear

Illustrated by Kevin Waldron

With additional verse by Angela McAllister

SIMON AND SCHUSTER

London   New York   Sydney

The Owl and the Pussycat went to sea

In a beautiful pea-green boat,

They took some honey,

and plenty of money,

Wrapped up in a

five pound note.

The Owl looked up to the stars above,

And sang to a small guitar,

"O lovely Pussy!

O Pussy, my love,

What a beautiful Pussy you are,

You are,

You are,

What a beautiful Pussy you are."

Pussy said to the Owl,

"You elegant fowl!

How charmingly sweet you sing.

O let us be married, too long we have tarried;

But what shall we do for a ring?"

They sailed away,

for a year and a day,

To the land where the Bong-tree grows.

And there in a wood a Piggy-wig stood

With a ring at the end of his nose,

His nose,

His nose,

With a ring at the end of his nose.

"Dear Pig, are you willing

to sell for one shilling your ring?"

Said the Piggy, "I will."

So they took it away,

and were married next day

By the Turkey who lives on the hill.

They dined on mince,

and slices of quince,

Which they ate with a runcible spoon.

And hand in hand,

on the edge of the sand,

They danced by the light of the moon,

The moon,

The moon,

They danced by the light of the moon.

Soon two became four,

then children galore,

Were climbing the Bong-tree all day.

They rattled the Turkey who lives on the hill,

With their noisy, rumbustifus play.

Pussy sighed, "My Dear,

there's no room for us here."

The Owl, with a nod, did agree.

So as clouds drifted by,

they took to the sky,

Floating over the shimmery sea,

The sea,

The sea,

Floating over the shimmery sea.

For Jack, Anna and Natalie
MM

For Tom and Charlie Mumford
and for Siwan
AA

ORCHARD BOOKS
338 Euston Road, London NW1 3BH
Orchard Books Australia
Level 17/207 Kent Street, Sydney, NSW 2000

First published in 2006 by Orchard Books
First published in paperback in 2007

ISBN: 978 1 84616 488 0

Text © Margaret Mayo 2006
Illustrations © Alex Ayliffe 2006

The rights of Margaret Mayo to be identified as the author
and of Alex Ayliffe to be identified as the illustrator
of this work have been asserted by them in accordance
with the Copyright, Designs and Patents Act, 1988.

A CIP catalogue record for this book is available from the British Library.

10 9 8 7 6 5

Printed in China

Orchard Books is a division of Hachette Children's Books, an Hachette UK company.
www.hachette.co.uk

Margaret Mayo & Alex Ayliffe

ROAR!

ORCHARD

Bold **lions** love roar, roar, **roaring**,
While cubs play – racing, chasing,
Scrambling over lionesses and – oops! – tumbling.
So **roar**, bold lions, **roar!**

Wrinkly **elephants** love **mud-wallowing,**

Squishy-squashy! Squishy-squashy! Squelching,

Trunks sucking and – shwoo-**oosh!** – water squirting.

So **wallow**, wrinkly elephants, **wallow!**

Stripy **zebras** love **fast galloping,**
Dumm-dd-dum! Hooves drumming,

Manes rippling, tails flying.
So gallop, stripy zebras, gallop!

Fierce **tigers** love prowl, **prowl, prowling,**
Through the jungle slowly slinking,

Softly creeping, no . . . grr . . . growling.
So **prowl**, fierce tigers, **prowl!**

Tall **giraffes** love stretch, stretch, stretching,
Long necks going up...up...reaching,

Black tongues flicking, lips leaf picking.
So stretch, tall giraffes, s t r e t c h!

Cheeky **monkeys** love swing, swing, **swinging,**
Hanging, dangling, tightly clinging,

Treetop scampering, calling and screaming.
So swing, cheeky monkeys, **swing!**

Plump **hippos** love swim, swim, **swimming**,
Floating, underwater strolling,
And opening their giant mouths ...**waaaahh**
...till all their teeth are showing.
So swim, plump hippos, **swim!**

Spotty **leopards** love climb, **climb**, **climbing,**
Up tree trunks zipping, sharp claws gripping,
Among the green leaves, crouching, hiding.
So **climb**, spotty leopards, **climb!**

Giant **pandas** love munch, **munch**, **munching**,
Bamboo seeking . . . bamboo finding,
Leaves chew, chewing, tough stalks grinding.
So **munch**, giant pandas, **munch!**

Bouncy **kangaroos** love jump, **jump**, **jumping**,
Hopping, bounding and . . . bumpety-bumping!
Little joey in the pouch, eyes peeping.
So **jump**, bouncy kangaroos, **jump**!

Grizzly **bears** love **fish, fish, fishing,**
In fast rivers splishing, splashing,

Paws catching, jaws quickly snatching.
So fish, grizzly bears, **fish!**

At night some animals love peaceful sleeping,
In a tree, on the ground or jungle floor.
But some are out prowling, hunting and eating,
While . . . wide-awake lions still love to **ROAR!**